Marc Yamaguchi

Suggested Cataloguing Data
Title: Arai Guma / Marc Yamaguchi, illustrated by Hung Hong, edited by Catherine Raine
Names: Yamaguchi, Marc, author | Hong, Hung, illustrator | Raine, Catherine, editor
Description: Arai Guma was first circulated in its manuscript form on YouTube as a web-series.
Identifiers: ISBN 9781738045402 (print) | ISBN 9781738045419 (ebook)
Subjects: LCSH: Raccoon--Fiction. | LCSH: Food security--Fiction. | LCSH: Environmental degradation--Fiction. | LCSH: Migration, Internal--Fiction. | LCSH: Families--Fiction. | LCSH: Identity (Psychology) in adolescence--Fiction. | BISAC: YOUNG ADULT FICTION / Animals / General | BISAC: YOUNG ADULT FICTION / Action & Adventure / General | BISAC: YOUNG ADULT FICTION/ Satire

Illustrations & Book Cover by Hung Hong

Book Design by Niki Hoi

First edition 2023

To the sentient beings whose future

we have borrowed from

FOREWARD

Marc Yamaguchi is nothing if not an optimist. He's also pretty much an adult-sized kid with an affinity for silly hats, playing in the dirt, and shamelessly anthropomorphising Toronto's ubiquitous trash pandas. Granted, the Japanese name for racoon, *arai guma*, or hand-washing bear, is much cuter. Still. If they needed a PR man, (and they do), they'd call Marc.

I met Marc over a decade ago, when I interviewed him for a story I was writing for the Globe and Mail newspaper about the planet-saving magic of rain gardens. I've since discovered, that like a well-constructed rain garden, the man has many layers.

He's a professor of English at Centennial College (that I knew), with a Masters of Environmental Education and Communication (that I did not know), and perhaps most importantly, he's an environmental activist – he's a David Suzuki Foundation Home Grown National Park Ranger (yup, there's a hat for that!) and the 2016 poster boy for (what else?) the magic of rain gardens.

And his newest layer? Writer of a young adult illustrated novel starring a family of country racoons – climate refugees – forced to migrate to the city to survive. On the surface, *Arai Guma* is a clever graphic novel – equal parts dark and funny – but dig a little deeper and it's an allegory for our troubled and uncertain times. So, is there a happy ending, you ask? I won't say. But Marc is the father of two young girls who will one day inherit this earth, so perhaps it's enough to repeat an old refrain: where there's life, there is hope.

– Signe Langford

Author of *Happy Hens & Fresh Eggs: Keeping Chickens in the Kitchen Garden with 100 Recipes*

PREFACE

The fall of 2023 marks five years since I graduated with a Masters of Environmental Education and Communication, and frustrated young climate activists continue to make headlines, and lately, it was for their arrest in tagging the Brandenburg Gate in Berlin, Germany. This event had made me wonder how Sweden's Greta Thunberg would have taken the news. She is the unmistakable and indefatigable young adult who continues to organize climate change protests. During our residency, my peers and I marveled at Thunberg's conviction, but we were troubled with a subtle and collective helplessness that played into an emerging sense of alienation and grief. None of us, however, was willing to give up the good fight because we were raising children, or were planning to raise families, or were teaching students for a living.

Arai Guma is the Japanese name for raccoon and is directly translated as *hand-washing bear*. The basic premise of *Arai Guma* is about a family of rural raccoons who is forced to migrate to the city and become embroiled in an ensuing food shortage there. The crux is that desperation consumes the animal population in the city so that individuals cannot see beyond their next meal. Those with more progressive ideals and the desire to strengthen their community come into conflict with the more entrenched power structures, which buttress the status quo. *Arai Guma* speaks to the angst in environmentalists of all ages, keeps the conservation going, and aims to inspire behavioural change. But *Arai Guma* really is an ode to the young adults who represent our best chance for meaningful change. Hopefully, it puts bounce in their step and nourishes their drive for a bright and sustainable future.

– Marc Yamaguchi

Creator and Author of *Arai Guma*

ACKNOWLEDGMENTS

My sincere gratitude to my illustrator, Mr. Hung Hong, who drew these imaginary beasts with his unique brand of visual whimsy. My humble thanks to my editor, Dr. Catherine Raine, who vetted the manuscript, safeguarded the humanity and preserved the humour in the text. Finally, my heartfelt appreciation for the support of my talented and generous colleagues at Centennial College in Toronto, Canada, who boosted my agency and honored my urgency to publish this young adult novel which is imbued with fierce optimism.

INTRODUCTION

What if your government locked up the discarded food your children need to keep from starving? This scenario is not speculative for the parents of five raccoon cubs, Rose and her mate, who are struggling to provide in conditions of extreme scarcity. As readers of their story soon learn, municipal powers have devised a compost bin with a locking lid to foil scavengers like Rose, who have been driven from their rural habitat by earth-devouring excavators. Refugees of suburban sprawl, Rose, Dad, Ray, Rachel, Ricky, Rory, and Ralph face internal conflict, separation, danger, and pain with dignity and grit.

Despite the grim social context, humour and affection animate the pages of *Arai Guma* thanks to its entertaining dialogue sprinkled with neologisms that express its inhabitants' unique worldview. (A glossary is provided to acclimatize readers to *Arai Guma*'s lexicon). Complementing the vivid language, Hung Hong's comic illustrations depict each character's individuality with heart and perception. For example, Hong's drawing of Rory perched with pilfering intent on a trash can lid, one paw insufficient to cover his smirking grin, instantly conveys Rory's signature "Sorry, Not Sorry!" attitude.

Immersion in the alternate universe of *Arai Guma* is a literary experience humans should not miss. Seeing "our" city from the perspective of raccoons gives us access to a mirror angled to reflect our wasteful, denial-ridden, and selfish ways. However, *Arai Guma*'s cautionary tale is ultimately an uplifting one in which communal values and empathy triumph over greed. As we root for big sister Rachel's quest to Turn the Green-wheely's lock, worry about the Youngins, and boo the Machiavellian Severn, we become emotionally invested in the fate of not only *Arai Guma*'s heroes and villains but also gain visceral awareness that we must care for an increasingly vulnerable natural world on whose health our own survival depends.

– Catherine Raine

Editor of *Arai Guma*

GLOSSARY

Advisor (4 of the 12 Inner Guard, in charge of 2 battalions of Sentries/Pledges)

Battalion (8 in total, each comprised of 2 companies that are run by a Sentry)

Chamber (Severn's personal lair)

Companies (comprised of 20 Pledges formed as separate attack units)

City Councillor (owner of Chester the dog and politician who dislikes raccoons)

Green-wheely (organic waste green bin)

Inner Guard (the elite group of 12 protecting and conspiring with Severn)

Pledge (young male recruit competing to open the green bin)

Rats' Alley (west end alleyway with overflowing green bins)

Sentry (8 of the 12 Inner Guard, run 2 companies of Pledges each)

Severnites (Severn's Army of Inner Guard and companies of pledges)

Stretchies (bungee cords)

Turner (a clever raccoon who can open a green bin)

Walkies (human beings)

Yard Guard (Chester the dog)

Yellow Caterpillars (construction vehicles used for excavation)

Youngins (raccoon pups, Rory and Ralph)

CHARACTER RELATIONSHIPS

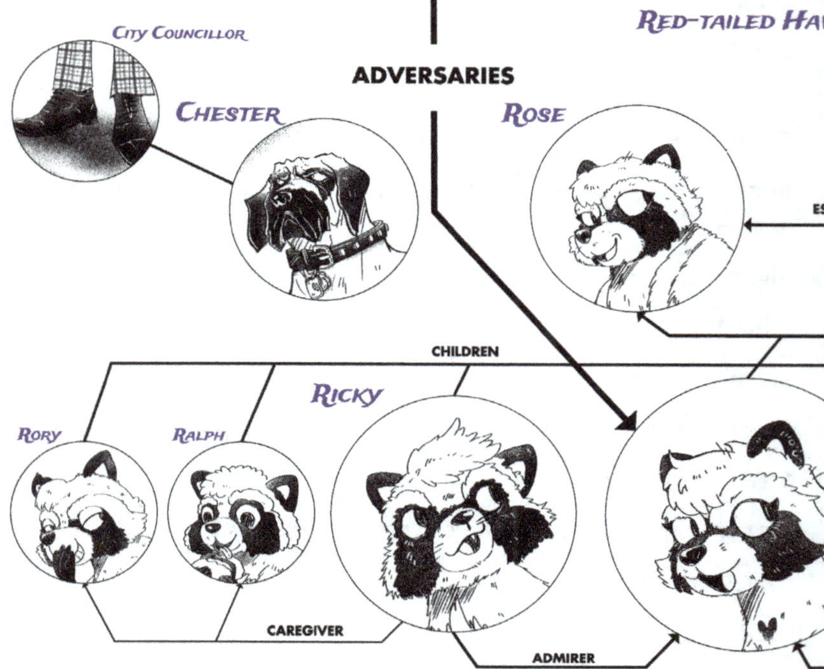

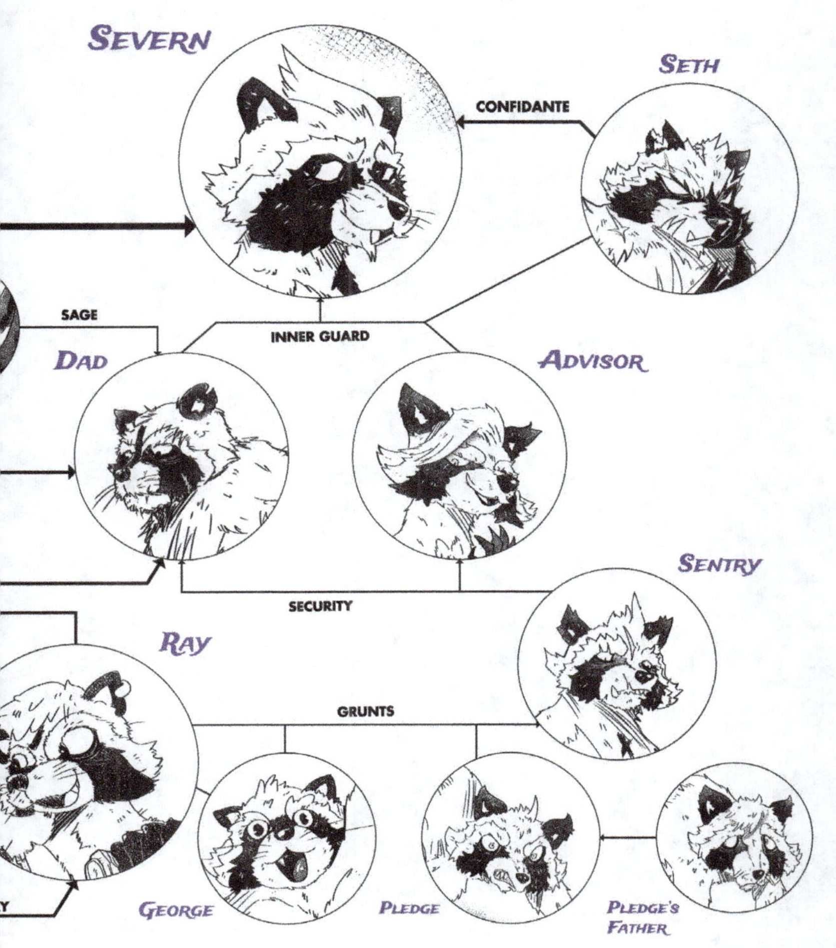

SEVERN
SETH
CONFIDANTE
SAGE
INNER GUARD
DAD
ADVISOR
SECURITY
SENTRY
RAY
GRUNTS
GEORGE
PLEDGE
PLEDGE'S FATHER

CONTENTS

The Family Finds Food

1st Born, Ray

Chapter 1

Rangers in the Night

Drip, drip, drip.

The streets were slick and flowing with the first flush of gutter debris that eventually caused the storm drains to back up, and the news had forecasted more rain to come. The heavy downpour of rain would release all kinds of smells that animate a neighbourhood so that terrestrial creatures could tell who was passing through and who was local.

From the safety of their old Red Oak tree, a family of raccoons groggily waited for a lull in the weather. The cubs Rory and Ralph began to putter about, but their older siblings Ricky, Rachel and Ray sat still, focused intensely on the twilight of the overcast sky. They went about their food scavenging no matter what. Their mother Rose had raised them with the saying, "You can't only walk on sunny days."

Rain or shine, it was time for the games to begin. Even the laggards Rory and Ralph had to admit that they looked forward to the start. Winners affectionately referred to their prizes as *green beans* – a family expression that represented the delight in something that suddenly revealed itself. Before the young brothers got a jump on the others, Rose reminded them to stay close together. Rory could be supercilious at times, and he would say "Green beans!" in a sarcastic tone to get on the others' nerves.

Ricky, Rachel and Ray were oblivious to the murmurings taking place between their mother and the troublemakers. The older siblings had their own ideas about mitigating the impact of this dead wood on the family. Still, they never defied their mother because mother knows best. Always take care of your own: be loyal to the cause but loyal to the family most of all. That rule was as golden as the fall sun that was now cutting a crisp skyline of the city crawling with commuters on their way home.

Rachel suggested to Ray that she take the lead and leave Ricky to whip the youngins into shape. This would allow Ray to effectively gauge the strength of the opposition. By default, Ricky was the cubs' disciplinarian. None of the offspring had ever really known their father. "No time to feel sorry for ourselves," thought Rachel, "Rory and Ralph had best fall in line." Rachel had more important designs for the family that required her concentration.

The opposition could lay as many boulders, noisemakers and

traps as they liked, yet Rachel was equal to the challenge and over-
came such obstacles without fail. Ricky, on the other hand, felt taking
care of the youngins came naturally to him. Ricky liked the predict-
ability of Rory and Ralph's antics, which made it easy for him to nip
their foolishness in the bud. Ray was too impatient and ambitious to
even consider sharing Ricky's role as a night-care provider.

Ray was focussed on winning and would often rub his hands
together like the adults who seemed to delight in stealing from their
opponents and aggravating them. As per Ray's calculations, the
object of the game was to get in and get out, so nobody got caught.
This was no simple feat. To look after himself was one thing, but
to honour his promise to his mother was another. Rory and Ralph
should have been cut loose long ago, and if it weren't for Ricky these
imps would have been roadkill by now.

Rose fully understood this was a dangerous game, but she was
neither slouch nor pushover. If you have ever seen a mother bear discipline her cubs, Rose could be ten times as fierce. To begin with, her
eyes would blaze with such fury that they would animate the very
night itself. The beautiful mascara lines she was born with would crin-
kle into extreme, jagged edges that accentuated matriarchal men-
ace. She had managed to keep this family safe until now with common sense values and the occasional bout of rage.

5th Born, Rory

A smorgasbord of riches awaited them five hundred raccoon lengths from their perch. Rose reminded her kids to warm themselves up with a thorough stretch first, but as soon as they began to slink down from their hollowed-out burl, Rory whined that his legs ached from the last family outing. Rose hissed, "Can it!" Rose was not self-conscious in the least. This periodic demonstrative correction was the kind of upbringing suited for this most dangerous place, the city.

Rose felt others could go ahead and judge her brand of old-school upbringing all they wanted; she had confidently taught all five fur babies to never to feel ashamed of who they were. Ricky, for example, was particularly receptive to his mother's praise. Ricky would look directly at a defiant Rory or Ralph when one of them dared question him with an adversarial, "What?!" by smiling condescendingly back at them like the Cheshire Cat and reply, "Remember, mother knows best."

Ray signalled to Rachel that the driveway across the street was perfectly cloistered for the heist they were about to pull off. Rachel stealthily moved to the head of their caravan to let their mom know they had zeroed in on the target. Rachel was her mother's favourite. Never one to confuse business with pleasure, Rachel was an alpha who commanded respect even from the opposition. She had never lost a game and tonight would be no different, or so she thought. With Ray on the lookout, it was up to Ricky to get those weak links in the chain across the street safely and up the driveway to their destination.

By this time, everyone was salivating over the imminent spoils that infused the air with notes of roast chicken. Rory was so impulsive that when he jumped the queue, he forgot about how rough Ricky could be with discipline. Ricky had an explosive temper that threatened to turn warning slaps into vicious blows. He might have permanently maimed his little brother if it weren't for Rachel's one sharp screech to stop what he was doing immediately and come to her.

Rachel was literally her mom's right-hand; Rose's arm had been broken in a life-or-death fight a few months ago, and it had never set right, so it was up to Rachel to run the family business. Like always, Rachel had to think quickly on her feet this night. Two new bungee cords straddled the Green-Wheely's latch. Only Ricky had sharper teeth than her, so she called him over to help her cut the Stretchies. Ray was at the ready, for as soon as they had finished gnawing through the cords, he would throw in his weight to tip the balance in their favour.

Unfortunately, it is the curse of youth that danger may be seen

The Yard Guard

head on but not from the periphery. While Rachel and Ricky were working on the Green Wheely's lid, and Rose and Ray looking on, Ralph raced Rory back down the driveway out of boredom for having to wait around. Ralph was roly-poly but had a leg up on his brother for once. Ralph would have won the race back to the tree-lined fence they had started from if it hadn't been for a contractor's pickup truck speeding by the moment Ralph stepped out onto the road.

Rachel and Ricky simultaneously snapped off the Stretchies as Ralph met his fate under the pickup's front left tire. Rory ran back towards his family in such a fright he crashed full force into the Green-Wheely, knocking it over on its side. Stunned, Ray didn't know whether to laugh or cry. Rachel's steely personality prevented her from being distracted by the black comedy; she had to take con-trol of the situation as best she knew how. She tightly gripped the black turn-handle of the Green-Wheely and threw her body weight into the Turn. She rejoiced that it cooperated as it had done before at other sites. Rachel was still the undisputed champion of the Turn. Their mother Rose gave the command to collect the spoils before the opposition discovered the breach in security. She snapped at Rory, who was still sobbing, and he clumsily gathered what he could.

The remaining five city rangers were solemn as they finished the victuals from the safety of their tree. Normally, the pack would have been savouring their victory by chittering away. But with Ralph gone, grief swallowed the family's usual banter and Rose's anguish was felt in her silence. It was small consolation that the deluge that had begun shortly after their return kept the opposition's dogs off their trail. The rainfall was deafening as the eaves overflowed and down-spouts rang out in a cacophony of steady noise. But Rachel thought she could hear her mother saying under her breath, "You can't only walk on sunny days."

The Yellow Caterpillars Take the Countryside

Chapter 2

Paradise Lost

Rachel's head bobbed in a catatonic-like state of dreaming as the sultry evening wind gently rocked the branch on which she was sleeping. Her dreams wove surreal images and sounds of her absentee father mumbling to himself. She could scarcely remember what he looked like, but the fights between her shadowy father and her mother Rose lived in her memory because they always ended the same way. Rachel could clearly remember seeing his haunches; he would exit the den as if in retreat, but in reality he had undisclosed business to tackle.

In the days before Rachel's father left and Rachel's little brother died, every evening the family would rise, and Rose would tend to Rachel's youngest siblings who stirred with hunger while Rachel would pretend to wake up for the same reason. Rachel would often be ruminating before anyone had woken up, but she instinctively knew not to trouble her mother, especially after her parents had argued. Rose's agitation would be tinged with sadness and regret;

2nd Born, Rachel

she could not turn her husband. However, Rose was not one to dwell on her troubles, and she relied on the same energy that erupted in fights to organize her cubs and ensure they stayed on the straight and narrow.

It was never a burden to follow her mother because Rachel prided herself on being indispensable to the family, like when she helped Ricky look out for the youngest cubs, who could barely balance walking the fence lines. They constantly needed reminding of the dangers of crossing backyards, which was exhilarating for young boys trying to make a name for themselves as fearless adventurers. Their older brothers, however, would taunt them into compliance and poke fun at their enthusiasm.

"Father will put us in the hunt ahead of Ricky and Ray!" said Rory confidently.

"When you trigger those Walkies' night lights, it's showtime," said Ray.

"Yeah, you're the main event hauled off in the Raccoon Removal van," smirked Ricky.

"Knock it off!" hissed Rachel, startling her mother, who was surveying the neighbouring properties for signs of danger. Rachel knew Rory and Ralph were still impressionable, and being misled by their older brothers could cost them their lives. Rachel wondered when and how her father had been misled. She often caught her mother muttering something about her husband being misinformed as she returned to wake up her two litters for evening excursions. In hushed tones, her mother would finish the conversation that her father had abandoned, and Rachel would lie dead still in order to gain perspective on their situation. It never occurred to Rachel that her mother was talking quietly to herself to escape the loneliness.

When the couple finally made the decision to migrate to the city a couple of years before, Rachel's father appeared to have made the right call to raise their family there. The countryside was under assault by the giant, yellow creepy crawlies that kept streaming in like a scourge upon their habitat. Predators and prey alike dropped their ancient feuds and ran for cover – if they could find cover. Rachel's father had rebuked his wife for wanting to wait out the storm of events that were rapidly changing their environment. He pointed out that the family never would have made it to safety without the help of a primeval foe, the Red-Tailed Hawk.

Unlike her parents, Rachel was born in the city, where they fled after humans had ransacked their rural home. She was a precocious cub, but she was nearly killed by a hawk in the city when she foolishly allowed it to catch sight of her. Rachel's mother would have severely reprimanded her for putting herself in harm's way, but her father

The Proclamation by Red-Tailed Hawk

defended the predatory hawk out of gratitude to its kin for once hav-

ing saved his family from harm. Although Rose argued her point with

customary forcefulness, her mate insisted on his way and to his sur-

prise prevailed. However, Rachel's father's victory was short-lived,

and the angry conversation turned into the loudest shouting match

between her parents Rachel could remember. Much more serious

than a passing squabble about parenting methods, this argument

had its roots in the past.

About a month before the excavation and utter upheaval of the

countryside, her father inadvertently scavenged in bushes too close

to a tree with a hawk's nest. Her father was unaware until he was

knocked over with a horrible burning sensation on the fleshy part of

his back. A hawk's wings fluttered wildly before establishing a safe

trajectory in which to land on a bough above and across from her

father.

Rachel's father could hear the bird laughing and cajoling him to

come out into the clearing of the forest floor so that they could have

a good look at each other.

"Come, come, tubby. I can't carry you off for a meal – your girth

is more than I can bear." The hawk continued, "Kills have been far

too easy of late. You were too good to be true."

Rachel's father had a bad wound from the hawk's talons, but he felt he was no longer in any danger.

"What gives, hawk? Your kind attack but don't talk. Is this some kind of trick?" asked her father.

"No trick, my weighty friend. Since you won't be joining me for supper, I may as well give you and your fellow striped simpletons some advice. You all would be better off moving far away from here," the hawk replied, impressed by his own magnanimity.

Her father wanted the hawk to elaborate, for he was keen to know why he should follow the advice of an enemy. Rachel's father was from the older generation who had it drilled into them to never question "authority." Rachel's father had also resigned himself to listen to Red-Tailed Hawk's lecture because he was curious about the hint of a mysterious and present danger.

The hawk's feathers were no longer ruffled, and he continued in a patronizing tone, "As you are keenly aware, *procyon lotor* has long sustained raptors, so I'd like to repay you this once. Knowing my penchant for good deeds, my relatives tell me I'm too generous for my own good. You may have noticed they've all but left for the city."

Rachel's father had stopped paying attention when the hawk started spouting Latin and words like "penchant." He hinted he had unborn mouths to feed and would be moving on, but the hawk suddenly swooped down to the ground within striking distance of Rachel's father. This time, the hawk made sure to speak slowly because it was common knowledge in hawk circles that raccoons had heads as dense as wood.

"Beyond that growing perimeter of Yellow Caterpillars you've conveniently ignored," the hawk took pains to explain, "is the city where the strongest and tallest grey trees scrape the sky."

Rachel's father lingered just long enough before the twitch of the hawk's eye scoped out its next unsuspecting prey. The hawk professed no love for the raccoon and pointed out bluntly that hawks saw fit to execute lives that suited their needs. Raccoons, on the other hand, were sadly predisposed hoarders with underwhelming figures as proof. It was why the hawk felt the city was a good fit for raccoons – creatures there had a tendency to store things in structures that were hardened and impermeable and full of compartments. This hawk was the last to join his brethren afar in the tall grey trees, which provided the perfect vantage point to pluck tenderlings from their nests or dens. Hawks have a wicked sense of humour by nature, and he shared this macabre detail with his unlikely friend.

"Raccoon, I tell you the truth because it's enlightened self-interest to respect the hierarchy of the food chain. I let you go and you propagate. Your children feed my children. It's rather elegant by design, don't you think?"

Rachel's father thought the hawk was rather in love with the sound of his own voice, but before he could reply the hawk lifted off as quickly as he had landed in front of him. The last words Rachel's father heard from the hawk was a fading and chilling shrill in the distance, "See you in the city . . . or you die-e-e-e-e-e."

As he watched the hawk fly towards the horizon, Rachel's father began to think about "the perimeter of Yellow Caterpillars" that were located in the same direction but not too far off in the distance. He had heard faint rumblings before and felt the earth quaking from time to time, but he had never connected the noisy and unsettling onslaught with the clever creatures who stood upright on their hind legs.

Rachel's father knew better than to impulsively bring news of this encounter to Rose. He tried to settle into the task of fishing at a familiar stream, but he could scarcely concentrate on bringing home sustenance for his pregnant partner, Rose.

"Yellow Caterpillars?!" Not only did Rachel's father scare away all the fish, but also he startled himself with his sudden exclamation.

Dad Is Distraught

Dad Scrounges Around for Bird Crumbs

Chapter 3

The Land of Grey Trees

Before Rachel's father went home to Rose, he was compelled to check the hawk's ominous prediction that the Yellow Caterpillars had metamorphosed into agents of death. As he came within a hundred yards of the site, Rachel's father could not speak or move as he witnessed the loss of paradise – butchery of everything he had known and on a scale unimaginable. The diesel exhaust singed the inside of Rachel's father's nose, and the rising sawdust from tattered trees blocked out the light from above, diminishing the canopy and creating an apocalyptic panic. There were horrific sounds of terror, altogether out of tune, which created a confusing image in Rachel's father's mind until he saw what was causing the earth to pulsate beneath his paws.

Once the chaos of fleeing animals and insects had died down, Rachel's father furtively made his way to the flank of ravaged and upturned earth, strange with its exposed roots. Bewildered by this upside down world that no longer resembled his home, he could not

Soon-to-be Mother Rose Loses Patience

make sense of the perfectly symmetrical and parallel tracks that had cleared the forest cover, leaving utter destruction in its wake. The remaining flora was shaking rhythmically as Rachel's father carefully peeked at the carnage.

He almost drew attention to himself when he mistakenly called out, "Hawk!" at the sight of a large bird swooping in. But this turkey vulture never saw Rachel's father because he was headed straight for a bloody jackpot that his carrion-bird gang had hit on. Among the dead, Rachel's father was horrified to see some coyotes who had been shot and subsequently driven into the ground by the Yellow Caterpillars – bulldozers and excavators that did not discriminate in their war on the forest nor its very rattled inhabitants.

Running back three farmers fields to their tree burl, Rachel's father burst open the makeshift door and mentioned for the first and last time the sight of the Yellow Caterpillars. Rose picked up on something otherworldly from the smell of her husband's paws, but he was too frantic to stop and spell out what he had witnessed. She thought she heard him muttering the words "Yellow Caterpillars," but Rose couldn't understand why something so innocuous as caterpillars had sent her mate into such a tizzy in their bucolic homestead.

Rose lunged and bit down hard on the tail of Rachel's father who shrieked in pain, but she could think of no other way to stop him from pacing wildly and disturbing the soft nesting materials. Rachel's father had made such a mess of Rose's carefully planned nursing area all the while muttering caterpillar this, caterpillar that. With her teeth still clenched tight around his tail, Rose screeched "ENOUGH!" which echoed throughout their hollow tree. Rose let go, and the couple sat motionless with only the sound of Rachel's father's blood dripping from his tail onto the leaf cover.

Although her mate had stopped pacing, Rose had never seen him worked up to such a degree. Her mate even shed tears as he explained what he had experienced, and he feared they would be buried alongside the coyotes that used to keep them up at night! Rose thought his chat with Red-Tailed Hawk was peculiar indeed, and she was inclined to dismiss both the bird's predictions and her mate's report of ecological catastrophe.

From the first mention of Rachel's father's encounter with Red-Tailed Hawk, she had scoffed at the validity of a predator imparting valuable information to a tree-hugging, hand-washing bear – since when did hawks and raccoons agree on anything, much less behave civilly towards one another? No raccoon had ever returned to speak of the land of tall grey trees, so a trek there seemed like an elaborate trap set by predators to lure their prey out into the open. Besides, it was common knowledge that hawks' heads were full of air.

A Severnite Advisor

Rose didn't want to believe her mate's story about the Yellow Caterpillars but would later concede her husband had been right to uproot the family and give birth to Rachel and her brothers in the city. The story of how Rose's favourite was born a city girl would begin with Rose making light of her husband's madness due to foraging for mushrooms. Rose didn't want to believe the gift of life came from a hawk's mercy.

That haughty bird, harbinger of traumatic events, came to represent disaster in Rose's mind, so Rose liked to blame it for her and her husband's ensuing irreconcilable differences. Projecting guilt on the raptor was a way to cope with her misery over the rapidly changing landscape and an environment fast becoming inhospitable to the original inhabitants. Being angry at a bird was less painful than experiencing the anguish caused by the loss of her home and beloved companion. Rose could usually repress memories of the day everything changed, but sometimes they came back and she couldn't stop remembering every word Rachel's father said.

"We must pack up and head for the city at once!" Rachel's father was doing calculations out loud about when Rose would give birth, but Rose struggled to understand what he was proposing. "Two months. No. One month. No, by two weeks, that's it! We've got to, we've got to, got to . . ."

Rose interrupted his frantic stuttering and looked him in the eyes.

"What's gotten into you? You're not making any sense. I'm the one who should be losing it, not you. I'm the pregnant one here!"

Rural raccoons considered the city a threatening place of mythical proportions, and Rose believed that those who broke with the countryside chased a dream that would result in tragedy. Rose was really annoyed he was going on this way about the city. Was this a bad joke?

"A hawk cut me pretty bad on my back, but instead of trying to take my life he stopped and said he felt sorry for our kind." Rachel's father was regaining his composure as he spoke at length. "The hawk wouldn't let me leave his kill-zone without first warning me that these Yellow Caterpillars would be the end of us if we stayed to watch their approach."

Rose was beginning to connect the dots, something about caterpillars being confused with great misfortune and extinction in her bird-brained husband. Was he out of his furry mind? In the first place, it was ludicrous to even consider he was talking with a hawk. If anything, he must have meant some know-it-all owl. Maybe if he got more oxygen, he would come to his senses.

"The Yellow Caterpillars have flushed out the hawk's prey in unbelievable numbers, which suits him fine, but he wanted me to know we'd only survive if we moved to a different kind of forest. A land that has very tall grey hardened trees. He wants our kind to survive only because he respects the food chain."

At this, Rachel's father let out a giant sigh and winced as he sat down on his hindquarters. The wound on his back from the hawk was still fresh, and as he curled up his tail, the matted fur pulled at the gash he got from Rose.

Rose took advantage of the pause in her mate's flood of words.

"Let's say you had a word or two with this known, silent killer. What makes you think a pregnant raccoon would leave the comfort of her home, travel with nothing but the babies in her womb, traverse the kill-zones of our enemies in order to reach the promised land that our friend, the hawk, calls the city?!"

When Rose made a point, she unashamedly began preaching with fervour, so nobody could get in a word edgewise. This night was different, however, and Rachel's father wouldn't give in until she agreed to come with him to see the desolation of the Yellow Caterpillars.

When Rachel, Ricky, and Ray heard stories about their parents'

Severn of the Severnites

past, it wasn't clear what made their parents sadder: the Yellow Caterpillars' desecration of the countryside, or that they had personally been forced from their home by the Yellow Caterpillars. On an extremely rare occasion, Rachel saw her father win an argument, like when Rose backed down on Rachel's punishment for failing to hide from the hawk that almost snatched her away in its talons. In fact, Rachel could only remember one other instance when her father exasperated her mother to the point that Rose gave in because she didn't have the patience to deal with his stubbornness. This was his decision to join a growing legion of city raccoons who had banded together to solve the "Green-Wheely" problem.

After living several months in the city, Rose began to get on Rachel's father's case concerning their dwindling stores of food. Rachel's father reminded Rose that their chances of surviving in the city were still significantly better than returning to the countryside to negotiate with the Yellow Caterpillars. But Rachel's father could never have predicted the Green-Wheely conundrum that was indiscriminately starving populations of city raccoons.

Not long before the arrival of the rural family of raccoons, some factions of urban raccoons decided to stop fighting over who ruled which neighbourhood, and they teamed up to solve this existential crisis created by the Walkies. The Walkies never fought fair; they stood upright, which gave them the upper hand. And the use of the Walkies' hands bestowed an advantage over other earthlings.

In truth, Rachel's father had been struggling to adapt to the new conditions of city life during their first year. As luck would have it, Rachel's father was recruited to help fatten the ranks of a raccoon gang in need of his girth. A large-sized raccoon projected an image of prosperity and wealth, and the gang's leader, Severn, equated wealth with power. Severn had great ambitions but was of modest proportions, so he would need enforcers on his quest to acquire resources and establish a prosperous economy that would secure his coronation.

For Severn's growing pack of raccoons, the perception of strength was extremely important. Hunger could be either a threat to his new order or a tool to manipulate the desperation of his followers. Severn turned them into troops to beat the Walkies at their game of starving the raccoons, and he was determined to outsmart the Walkies' Green-Wheely anti-theft technology. Severn judged the Walkies as contemptuous creatures for their senselessly wasteful ways – evidently, one animal's junk was another's treasure.

Ambition is born from envy, and the Walkies' largesse made Severn as green with envy as the newly impregnable green bins. If it had served Severn's purposes, he would have commanded Rachel's father and his coterie of enforcers to scratch out the eyes of the Walkies, those bi-pedal miscreants who routinely invaded his territory and robbed his kin of the refuse that should have fortified his expanding army.

Ricky Is Preoccupied with the Youngins

Chapter 4

An Education

Ricky missed his father even though their bond wasn't close, and a sense of unease made Ricky's back hunch up as he patrolled the high fence near the family's tree. Their father's absence made Ricky extra protective of his baby brothers, who were the cutest kits on the planet. The twins were born identical, but the difference in their character was as obvious as the difference in their weight. For one thing, Rory had a hankering for pacing like their father, which made him quite a bit slimmer than his brother Ralph. At sunrise, Rory would attempt to leave the tree den when the others fell asleep, so Ricky always had to keep an eye open. Yet this was manageable because the other twin was sedentary. In fact, Ralph preferred to be still; he would eat, sleep, relieve himself, and go back to sleep - full stop.

When Ricky thwarted Rory's attempts to leave, Rory would plot mischievous acts against his twin brother like jamming tree-bits up his nostrils, which caused Ralph to wake up and gasp for air. More

3rd Born, Ricky

devious were Rory's threats to "raccoon tip" the sleeping Ralph, who could fall prey to the Yard Guard sniffing about below. In these moments, Ricky wondered if Rory had inherited his macabre imagination from their mother, who used to warn the siblings that if they didn't smarten up, they could see how much they liked having the Yard Guard as their babysitter.

In Rose's first litter, Ricky was always first to concede and last to feed. He was generally a nice boy and didn't resent his mother's preference for Rachel and Ray to do the heavy lifting. Ricky saw himself as a homebody and thrived on Rose's praise. Ricky accepted he was best suited to look after the twins when the family needed to go out and scavenge for food. After all, Rachel was smart and could often anticipate their mother's instructions before Rose had finalized them in her head.

Ray, on the other hand, had the brawny attributes of his father, plus Ray was swift on his feet. Rose came to rely on Rachel and Ray's gifts for larger hauls. However, Rose was most affectionate with Ricky and thought if she nurtured his maternal instincts, Ricky would make the dandiest of dens for some lucky lady-sow.

Ricky escaped the watchful eye of Mother as long as he kept Rory and Ralph out of harm's way, or more precisely, out of Rose's way. Rachel and Ray were also grateful for Ricky's vigilance – the lit-

4th Born, Ralph

tle brats often trashed their makeshift maps that were laid out for Mother's approval. Rachel and Ray had a terrific synergy when they planned evening strikes, but Rachel had the edge once a plan was underway. Everyone in the family recognized Rachel's dexterity with her hands. Rachel may not have had Ray's physical size advantage, but she had learned to climb better and no thanks to her deadbeat father, Rose would add. More than anything, Rose respected Rachel's ability to think on the spot – she was graceful under pressure.

Ricky prided himself on his powers of observation, and he fancied that Rachel made an exceptional spy. In fact, Ricky was spying on the spy, and he was quietly delighted by what she was up to now. Ricky never let Rachel know that he saw her frequently tail her brother Ray, who was returning home inexplicably later each night. Rachel would control her breathing before sneaking back in the den just ahead of Ray.

Ricky would keep his eyes tightly shut, but his nose detected faint, foreign smells on his brother and sister. The odour was more noticeable on Ray, so Ricky guessed their secret excursions were related, but they were not necessarily co-conspirators. Ricky never confronted his siblings about his suspicions because if the conversation went sideways, he would feel responsible for undoing the relative equanimity the family had been enjoying since their father had

Rose, the Matriarch

left the den half a year earlier.

A single parent like Rose can be forgiven for overlooking her kids' basic hygiene now and then. It wasn't that she was negligent, but since her mate had seemingly abandoned the family, Rose was provider, teacher, defender and executioner. She was also the family bookkeeper, and she began to think there was something more to Ray's sudden growth spurt than the activation of adolescent hormones. When Rose confronted Ray about him filling out like a bear in November despite the family barely being able to find sustenance, Ricky almost let it slip that Ray's BO was increasingly intolerable, too. Ray didn't bother to tiptoe around the lie any longer because something bigger was at play.

Ray lambasted his mother, "Father has been showing me how to make it in the city, and a country pumpkin like you just wouldn't understand."

Ray would have continued with an insult about Rurals being stuck in the dark ages, but Rose shut him up with her left paw coming down hard upon his snout. Ricky was aghast and paralyzed by their mother's violent reaction to Ray's insolence. Ray would have received matching scars on his cheeks if Rachel hadn't jumped between them just in time.

Rachel's voice broke the tension, "Mother! I'm just as guilty for leaving the den without your permission."

Rose felt betrayed. With her nostrils flaring, her eyes flashing, her mouth uttered one word, "Why?!"

Rachel, the Family's Next Turner

Rachel Has an Idea

Chapter 5

The Pledge

Silence ensued after Rachel's admission, so Ricky positioned himself closer to Rachel, Ray, and Rose who were further down the tree from him. As much as Ricky didn't want to miss any more big reveals, his priority was to provide Rose with moral support like he did when she would have regrets about giving up everything to follow her mate to the city. This time, Ricky could tell that his mother's controlled rage threatened to explode into violence, so he resisted his instinct to verbally console her.

Ricky looked back at Rory and Ralph, who were innocently dreaming about garbage feasts. But their dreams could not have been further from the reality of this family crisis, which threatened to destroy the trust needed to secure food to eat. He sensed Rose's hurt over Rachel's double-betrayal: her surprise defense of Ray and the boar who fathered all five kits. Who was this new sister, the former Mama's girl now implicated with the disgraced patriarch? Rachel broke Ricky's train of thought with a confession.

A Hungry Pledge

"Mother, Ray has been training to overtake the Walkies and restore balance to the food chain. He's been meeting with rival raccoons to break into the Green-Wheelies that have deprived our community of the right to eat!"

It's rare to see so many raccoons huddled together at daybreak, but Rachel's stunning revelation meant no one was keeping track of time. On a normal day with fewer emotions clamouring for her attention, Rose might have appreciated this development as a sign of good news. Rose had felt defeated by the Walkies' invention ever since its introduction, and she was stricken with guilt for failing her family, especially the two little ones. However, Rose's uncharacteristic listlessness made Rachel grow up in a hurry. Rose's sense of doom made Rachel thirst for more knowledge and emboldened her to take more calculated risks to save their family from starvation.

While Rose grappled with Rachel's betrayal, Ray was stewing in his own juices after the humiliating blow to his face. Ray reacted by pinning his anguish on his sister, and he took pleasure in imagining how easily he could knock Rachel off her perch and deprive her of their tree's protection. Ray had been wronged, and now Rachel had spoiled the secret he was sworn to protect – she must have been bloody spying on him. She was weird, she was jealous of him. She was probably dropped on her head as a cub, which explained why she gave so many blank stares.

As Ray's tears began to wash away the blood-stain on his muzzle, he all at once shouted at Rachel, "What the fang did you say that for?!"

Rachel was caught off-guard, but at these words Ricky hurried back up to the sheltered fork of the tree and hushed Rory and Ralph who had cried out in alarm. After Ricky had soothed the boys back to sleep, he could eavesdrop on what was being discussed by Mother, Rachel, and Ray. Looking down at them, they seemed to be talking about feeding the family of six, but this was far more ominous.

After Rachel regained her composure, she spoke again, keenly aware of how delicate the situation was between her, her brother, and their mother. If their emotions got the better of them, they might forfeit their seclusion in their tree situated in a Walkie's back-yard. That would certainly jeopardize the lives of the youngins, Rory and Ralph, who could not outrun the indiscriminate cruelty of the Walkie's Yard Guard.

Rachel confronted Ray, "Get a grip, Ray. Come clean. Are you really a Pledge?"

Ray growled back, "Shut your double-crossing, ringworm mouth!"

Rose was still struggling to process the news being delivered

A Severnite Sentry

piecemeal, so Ray's profanities didn't even register in her head.

Rachel persisted, "Tell us you haven't been initiated. Tell us Father would have stopped your hazing."

At the mention of their father, Rose snapped out of her daze and shot a look at Ray, demanding to know more, "Ray, your father hasn't been seen for months. Has he got something to do with this?!"

With a gentle push of her nose, Rachel nudged her mother's shoulder, a compassionate gesture that asserted Rachel's new role as the leader of the pack. She had become a guide, the family diplomat, and with the calm but confident voice of a peacemaker she argued, "Ray, as long as you aren't initiated, it's not too late. Father may belong to Severn, but you still have your freedom."

Ray thought this was highfalutin talk.

"Freedom, Rachel?! Who died and made you the preacher?" Ray continued, "We've been struggling to feed Rory and Ralph, never mind us. Those Walkie bastards! We never took more than we needed. We eat their scraps. And then, they even hoard the garbage. I'm proud of Father. He's doing something about it. He's not compost-for-brains. There's strength in numbers. Severn has nearly all the clans on his side now. He's getting the best of the best to pledge. Severn has a Green-Wheely in his possession, right now, and we're vying to be the next Turners!"

Rose looked from Rachel to Ray in confusion, having never heard Severn's name before, the revelation that Severn had brought a large number of raccoons onto his side, and the fact that she was receiving second-hand news on the whereabouts of the children's father. She was demoralized by how out of touch with city life she was. Maybe Ray was right about her useless sentimental attachment to the country-side. He and Rachel had adapted so much better than her, and their maturity made her feel insignificant. Rose had never seen her children have a heavy-duty conversation like this before.

Rachel took a long pause before speaking again to let Ray recover his dignity. He was proud to belong to such a forward-thinking society that validated his desire to be treated as an adult raccoon. Unfortunately, Ray was so consumed by the rituals of Severn's growing legion of go-getters that he hadn't actually figured out how to open a Green-Wheely. Rachel was now conscious of Ricky listening to the argument as intently as their mother, but Rachel still had one more important revelation to make. Night was on the cusp of becoming day, and Ray had nearly talked himself to sleep, so Rachel felt this was an opportune time to drop her own bombshell.

Rachel asserted, "Look, Severn is gaining power over more and more neighbourhoods, and it'll be a game-changer if a raccoon besides Severn can open a Green-Wheely. But every young male east of the river has failed the competition. What's up with that?"

Before Ray could warrant an explanation, Rachel announced with an intensity that made her unrecognizable to her own mother, "Tonight, I'm going to be this family's Turner."

Severn Gives a Rousing Speech

Severn's Confidante, Seth

Chapter 6

Severn's Lair

"Fat chance, you stinkin' sow!" Ray growled, and he would have knocked Rachel twenty-five feet to the ground had his mother not struck him first. Rose came down on his head with a double-fisted hammer blow, which caused him to bite his tongue so hard that Rose had now given him two wounds that bled.

"Your father may be a good-for-nothing boar, but I'll be damned if I raise a son to disrespect his family this way. Rachel, go on."

All eyes were on Rachel – this was the first time their mother had invited a sibling to speak at length. Rachel's heart raced like the pulse of a hungry woodpecker, but she calmed herself before speaking again.

"Look, I've watched Severn's Pledges mount the Green-Wheely and fail. I've seen them pin their hopes on the Turn, but they always become, what, just ordinary rank and file . . ."

Ray cut in. "You stay out of this. You know nothing of the selection process. Severn wants a winner. I've been waiting for my Turn, and I'm damn close now. I do this – we don't go hungry. We're gonna get . . . "

Ray's excitement suddenly faltered when he noticed his sister examining her front paws like she was more concerned about some imperfection she found there.

"Ray, Severn isn't expecting winners. Do you think he's smiling because he's expressing sympathy for the fathers who lose their sons to him?"

Rachel's suspicions weren't far off the mark. Severn's pledging system was an elaborate ploy to recruit the strongest and most ambitious young males from the city's neighbourhoods far and wide. Starving and desperate families, who had been thwarted by the locking mechanism of the Walkies' organic waste receptacles, begged Severn to teach them the ways of opening the Green-Wheely. At the beginning of every pledging ceremony, the Green-Wheely that Severn and his inner coterie had confiscated would be on display with the lid open to strike awe in the raccoons who had never seen the inside of one.

Since Severn had mastered the Green-Wheely, he was considered as clever as the Walkies; therefore, he called the shots. Only one other raccoon, his closest Advisor, had been taught the Green-Wheely's secret. Nobody dared disagree with this arrangement.

Severn promised that he'd educate the first-born males of every family if they committed their sons to the pledging ritual and entered his lottery for the chance to crack the Walkies' code. Every night the Green-Wheely would be reset out of sight, and then ten ambitious but clueless males were invited to climb up onto Severn's stage, a broad platform at mezzanine level set in an abandoned warehouse, and one at a time they would carry the weight of their families' hopes, their pride at stake.

While the stage was in plain view for all to see, this mezzanine prevented onlookers from noticing Severn's antechamber, which led to his private quarters in an abandoned boiler room. Rachel had discovered a perfectly protected bird's eye view of the facility from where she could see past a dense thicket of overgrown ivy which covered the exterior rear portion of the warehouse. She would carefully part the unkempt vegetation and look through the aperture of a broken window pane just beneath the roof's edge, which then allowed her to become familiar with the transitions that took place deep within this hollowed-out machine die factory.

Rachel watched the routine change of the guards below her, and each time she could catch the rising odour from the green bin that was wheeled out for the Pledges but ultimately confiscated again via the antechamber to the Green-Wheely's safehouse. As far

Dad Checks His Orders

as she could tell, no one entered that darkened hallway connected to the back of the mezzanine except Severn and an elusive raccoon who received the prized possession from the Advisors at the line of demarcation.

Rachel concluded this was no public hall; this was a fortress steeped in ritual with hints of punishment for anyone who dared step out of line or misunderstood the protocols. On the basement floor, the Pledges and their fathers formed a semi-circle that extended outwards from the base of the stage with rows upon rows of members clamouring to get a taste of the dream that had materialized before their very senses.

Rachel's concern for Ray's well-being wasn't the only factor that motivated her secret mission to spy on Severn's ceremonies; for some time, she had been worried about how her father was implicated in Severn's operation. Her father was nothing like Severn, who was of average build and had a svelte figure compared to him. Moreover, Severn seemed wiser given his proclivity for words and talent for recruiting followers with stirring speeches. Rachel's father struggled to hold a conversation with just one raccoon, much less a restless crowd.

While Severn had made many covet the Turn, not all raccoons accepted the invitation to pledge. There were murmurings of rac-

coons on the outskirts who did not believe Severn's promise of largesse. Severn viewed these raccoons as treebillies who were at the
mercy of a fluctuating supply of food. These simpletons also had no
appreciation for words, especially fancy ones that could impart the
values of solidarity and explain concepts like opportunity cost.

Rachel had never heard a raccoon project its voice so well. Even
from her position peering down through that lofty broken window
behind the staging area, she could hear Severn bellow with gravitas.

"My boys. There's a Turner among you yet. Do not be discour-
aged. Your fathers shall rejoice that you were pledged and now by
my side. Look around you!"

The dejected young male raccoons and their fathers would likely
have succumbed to the pangs of hunger and the humiliation of fail-
ure had it not been for Severn's call-to-arms. For this was more than
a distinguished brotherhood; this was an anthem for modernity, to
rise above their subsistence way of life and petty concerns.

"Scavengers no more! Our collective deters predators. Our alli-
ance means we own the night. Our communion defies the Walkies'
expectations!" Severn always finished his grandiose speeches by taking a dig at the Walkies. Then the fathers of the failed Pledges would
rush the stage. Severn's Inner Guard held the line and the pleas for
second chances would be ignored. As the chaos swirled around him,

Severn would exit the stage as gracefully as he had entered it.

The Inner Guard of twelve raccoons saw to it that nobody breached the secret sect. This elite unit was made up of eight well-built Sentries who would descend to the basement floor and stand between the crowd of onlookers while Severn's four large Advisors remained on the mezzanine. The Advisors would open and close around him like a curtain as Severn took to the front of the stage, and they looked down menacingly at the sorry lot of fools who sought entitlement in vain.

When the competition ended in the early hours of the morning, Severn's four Advisors brought forth the Green-Wheely that had been reopened so that the Pledges were left to salivate over the king's ransom. The Advisors barked out orders that looking was permitted but touching was prohibited. Still, the Pledges were enthralled with the contest and risked lingering after the order was given to go home. The young uninitiated male onlookers fantasized about their Turn. The following evening, new Pledges would leave their dens in haste, and arrive to find the Green-Wheely full of odorously steaming enticements that the Advisors would abandon at show time.

Rachel could see her father was counted among the Advisors, and they were the only other raccoons allowed to maneuver the Green-Wheely and stand with Severn on the upper stage. The eight

Sentries faced outwards and formed an outer arc in the lower bowl-shaped area of this pseudo auditorium that kept the Pledges at bay. The suspense was palpable until three Advisors dragged out the Green-Wheely from Severn's chamber for all to smell. Once on display, Ray's father would stand in front looking upon the Pledges below, and the other two Advisors would take positions on opposite flanks to intercept anyone trying to sneak a look from the sides. This was all Rachel could discern from her viewpoint.

But a fourth Advisor watched Severn's back in case of ambush, which let him look upon the Green-Wheely as freely as Severn did. This Advisor was Severn's confidante, second-in-command, and his name was Seth. It was Seth's job to call upon a Pledge each night to try his luck and open the Green-Wheely. One by one, night after night, the Pledges would fail. Young males have a particularly voracious appetite, and Severn and Seth knew they would be easily intoxicated by their proximity to the spoils.

Because the young males were hopelessly distracted from what they were doing, Seth would then corral the dejected aspirants backstage to conscript them into the battalion academies run by the Advisors. The Sentries would escort the last of the fathers and uninitiated Pledges to the entrance of Severn's Lair, repeat Severn's specious words of encouragement, praise the fathers' sense of duty,

Severn Lights up the Lair

and insist that they should be very proud of pledging their sons. The Sentries would then dutifully report their numbers to the Advisors.

One evening, not long before Rose learned the truth about Ray's nighttime forays, Severn called Ray's father to his side for a private chat after Ray and some other Pledges left to go back home. Severn knew Ray's father would leave his post from time to time to speak with his son briefly before sending him on his way, but Ray's father didn't realize that these short breaks had been noticed.

Ray's father was also unaware that Severn would often gaze upon his physique – the other Advisors were not as tall, nor as large in the paw. Nevertheless, the other Advisors were not to be under-estimated because they were skilled in combat and never strayed far from their master. Seth protested against Severn's invitation for Ray's father to join him for an exclusive tête-à-tête until Severn cajoled him.

"Come, come, young Ray will soon perform the rite of passage and make you wish he was your boy." At this, Ray's father could not conceal his pleasure at hearing Severn's compliment.

Severn continued directing his comments back to Ray's father, "I have faith in that boy of yours. He's been endowed with your size. He has the same determination I saw in you when we found you still collecting nuts like a scared little squirrel."

When the Advisors cackled, Severn closed the gap between himself and the jokers with lightning speed. If looks could kill, their lives were hanging by a creeper's vine.

"Go! Bring us the victuals, lock the Green-Wheely, and leave us!" Seth was smarting from being excluded, yet he dared not upset his master and did as he was told.

Severn resumed once the Advisors left the chamber, "You know, we animals mostly live in the present, in the now. But it's a mixed blessing, and if we do not gain mastery over our destiny, we are forever at the whims of others. Or their dinner."

Severn's chilling laugh made Ray's father wish he could have walked home with his son to strategize about the Turn, to laugh about the other Pledges' fathers who cheered a bit too much, and even to hear about Ray's siblings. Ray's father would ask about Rose and whether she could rely on their daughter to watch out for the young pups, Rory and Ralph. Somehow, Ricky wasn't going to be the son he had hoped for. He could talk to Ray about that, too, and tell him there was no rivalry for his affection there.

Suddenly aware of the silence, Ray's father realized he had never been left alone with the Master before, and he felt tongue-tied. Instead of rebuking Ray's father for not responding to his brilliant philosophical musings, Severn paused and then continued in a hushed tone.

"Tell me something. Do you know why you're an Advisor when you're really more of a Sentry?"

Severn sat back and then pointed his wiry finger at Ray's father.

"When I discovered and chose you for my inner circle, it wasn't for your sparkling conversation. My Advisors and I happened to see you hammering away at that residential bird feeder you had wrestled to the ground. I thought we could use that kind of muscle. My Advisors, however, wanted to brush you off. They thought you were pathetic for scrounging around for bird crumbs in our territory, and they ridiculed your story about a red-tailed hawk who supposedly told you to start over in the city. I'm rather fond of raptors. Forgive my Advisors for not seeing the big picture."

Severn glided closer to Ray's father like he was skating on ice. "You have a big boy – do you think he can master the Turn? Don't try to fool me. I know you think he can. He's next to press his luck. Or pull. Or whatever you've coached him to do."

Normally, Ray's father postured as the strong and silent type, but his nerves got the better of him when Severn insinuated Ray had inside information on the Turn. His monosyllabic "No" echoed so loudly in Severn's chamber that Seth, who was lurking just outside and straining to hear what was being discussed, leapt six feet in the air and landed on all fours like a cat caught stealing the family goldfish. The kerfuffle was loud enough for Severn to know Seth must have been listening to his conversation with Ray's father.

Severn was amused and resumed with gusto, "Come now. Take from the victuals over there." Seth was incredulous that his master would give Ray's father first dibs at the Inner Guard's spoils. As Ray's father collected a modest ration and began to leave, Severn pulled him close and added with guttural malevolence, "Don't let me down."

Rachel and Ray Have a Sibling's Quarrel

A Sentry on Guard

Chapter 7

Rachel's Secret

That night, Ray left the Lair without knowing his father had been summoned by Severn. In fact, Ray would have made it home sooner, but he had slowed down to examine the wild shrubbery poking through the fences of the alley.

"Ray!" said a familiar voice above him, which was so startling that he rolled over on his back in submission. Rachel emerged from her cloak of darkness, having inched closer atop the fence and become visible in the light cast by the lamppost.

"Oh, Geez! Rachel, you scared the scat out of me! Are you out of your furry freakin' mind?! What are you doin' here? You still tryin' to be our family's Turner by spying on me? Didn't the paw-lashing I got teach you not to test Mother?"

Ray would have gone on more about the vexing ways of meddling sisters, but Rachel shot him a discerning look that was eerily similar to their mother's.

"Ray, we've got to go back."

Ray objected they would risk waking up the neighbour-hood dogs, but Rachel shook her head and interrupted, "Take me back to Severn's chamber, and let me show you how to open the Green-Wheely."

This plan was more outrageous than Ray could stomach, and he began to sweat profusely. She may have been to Severn's Lair to witness the pledging, but how did she know about his guarded chamber? And since when did she get to call the shots? She had better think twice if she thought she was going to ruin his chances to be adorned by their father!

Having spent several nights watching Severn's machinations, Rachel had begun to notice how much Ray worshipped their father. Ray would always find a way to be near him during Severn's speeches. The two of them would speak softly to avoid drawing attention, and Ray would receive a morsel of food in secret. Rachel found it endearing to see her father express his love this way. She wished that her father could come home so that the other family members could see this side of him.

Rachel had escaped detection each night by leaving before Ray and the other Pledges were dismissed. On the night she told her family about Ray and their father, she had noticed something different. At the close of the ceremonies, as per his routine, Severn slipped into the darkness behind his Inner Guard. Before he had gone completely, Severn looked back upon his growing army with a smile so wide that the emerging light of the morning flashed against his immaculate teeth. Severn had paused just long enough for Rachel to make out the form of an antechamber more distinctly. Somewhere, back there in the shadows, was a private chamber housing the leader and guarding his treasure.

When Rachel couldn't get Ray to cooperate, she appealed to him on the grounds that their father was embroiled in something that reeked of trouble. Together they could still save their father and bring him home.

Ray reacted incredulously to Rachel's plea.

"What? Father need saving?! He's trying to save you and the rest of the family! Rachel, ugh! I might as well tell you."

Ray continued to patronize her.

"Listen up, little sister, I'm training to take Father's place. Ever since he left, Mother has been unable to secure our family's safety. We both know Ricky couldn't scare a butterfly. You still lookin' for an explanation about me takin' over? Wanna spell this out for Mother, too?"

Ray's smug expression showed satisfaction over regaining control of the situation. But time was running out, so Rachel spoke plainly.

"Ray, Severn serves himself and Father is being used. I've witnessed how jealous Severn's Advisors are and how he uses their insecurity to manipulate them. Look, we can talk about that later. Get me near that Green-Wheely, and I'll get 'er done."

Ray thought it hilarious to hear Rachel talking like a Pledge.

"Get 'er done?" he sneered at her, "Hmmph, you're talkin' bullscat. Boys bigger than me couldn't get 'er done, so what makes you think a puny pup like you can?"

Rachel knew more than he liked about his secret society, but instead of outing her as a spy to the Severnites, Ray thought he'd let her get her just desserts without him having to lift a paw. He would let her humiliate herself on the Green-Wheely. That would shut her up. Ray made Rachel swear on their father's life she would never speak to anyone about what she knew, and if she failed to open the Green-Wheely, she wouldn't get another crack at it.

"One shot is all. You follow my lead 'cause I have to sneak you in. Ha! You're already a pretty good sneak. You know, Father tapped me to become our family's breadwinner. He pledged *me*, right, and one day he figured me and him might open the Green-Wheely the way Severn and that other Advisor do it. What makes you so sure you can open it? Crawdads! Father's part of his Inner Guard and he's told me

Dad in Sumo Stance

where it's kept."

Ray was annoyed because he was sure his taunts would make Rachel chicken out and give up on infiltrating Severn's chamber. Much to Ray's chagrin, Rachel would not be dissuaded nor guilted into staying away. She was an exceptional pathfinder and had no trouble returning to Severn's Lair. She may have been smaller than Ray, but this made her lighter on her feet. Ray was out of breath when they reached a safe distance from which to view the pledging area.

Rachel motioned to Ray to come close to where she had watched him and the other Pledges on numerous occasions. Ray realized she had the perfect cover of a thicket of overgrown vegetation that leaned against the warehouse exterior. He carefully looked down through the broken window that was nearly twenty feet above Severn's orations but still within earshot since his voice would echo throughout his cavernous auditorium. From this vantage point, Ray could see how Rachel had been able to detect the antechamber that served as a narrow hallway leading to the entrance of Severn's private chamber. From here, Ray and Rachel were within range to catch the faint smell of the precious contents of the Green-Wheely.

Severn's speech from earlier that evening was still fresh in their memory.

"Brethren, lend me your ears." Severn relished the spotlight. "Fortune is shifting in our favour. A great many of you may not have become a Turner, but you are nonetheless soldiers who will guarantee our victory over this concrete jungle. We have evolved from our forest foraging cousins who have a naive view of the Walkies' benevolence. We will take back the night. The Green-Wheelies have destabilized our territorial pacts with the neighbouring regions of raccoons. Now, we are left to fight amongst ourselves in a revolting spiral to the bottom. The greedy Walkies have created this Tragedy of the Commons by taking more than their share of the Earth's bounty. But once we have brought our population under control and stamped out the pockets of resistance, we will feast courtesy of the Walkies' inflated sense of ego. Our triumph will make us owners of a new economy. The Severnites will be more than just its gatekeepers!"

As the siblings settled deeper into the thicket, they both sat in silence, presumably thinking about their next move. Ray was ruminating over Rachel's recent words, inwardly scolding her for not heeding his warnings and failing to appreciate how she had debunked the rigged competition. While Rachel did calculations in her head about the distance to the Green-Wheely and getting past the obstacles, Ray's unvoiced complaints turned to worries that the sunrise would soon lift their shroud of protection.

The Siblings Infiltrate Severn's Private Chamber

Rachel Avoids Detection

Chapter 8

The Turn

As was his custom, Severn retired to his private chamber following the rousing "Brethren" speech and comforted himself by pontificating and posturing in front of a reclaimed Walky full-length mirror. He hated being called a butcher; he despised the rape and pillage mentality that had plagued governance movements before. He wanted the Severnites to confront the scarcity of resources with precision and calculation, and those who yielded would be spared.

By incorporating more raccoons into his new economy, Severn would proselytize them. After all, demand was nothing without supply – a steady market of bottom feeders. He was a statesman, he was sophisticated, and he superseded his comely but out-of-step ancestors by manipulating systems for his own gain. Severn's reign would be an affront to Nature, which perpetually impoverished his species. Visualizing his stately head garlanded in gold, Severn's speech rehearsal soon tapered off into a deep self-satisfied sleep.

Rachel, however, could not indulge in egotistical reveries of conquest. She was laser-focussed on finding an opening in the fortress she had been studying from a distance. Now, their success would depend on Ray's knowledge of Severn's Lair from the inside. After Rachel had shown Ray her vantage point, he led them down to the front of the building. They turned the corner in tandem and stealthily raced past the main entrance, entering through the fire exit at the side of the building that was normally guarded against Pledges trying to jump the line.

With their backs against the wall, Ray and Rachel faced the pledging pit and side-stepped their way along it to the very back of the mezzanine. Ray told Rachel that this window of opportunity was their best chance to access the antechamber in which the Green-Wheely was whisked back and forth each night. They went unnoticed because the ceremonies that evening were long since over, the windows were shuttered, and half of the Sentries had been dismissed to get some shut-eye right before the other four were scheduled to replace them. It was so dark below that Ray and Rachel had to feel around with their paws for the rear staircase that Ray said they could climb to bypass the stage area altogether.

As they approached the antechamber, which led to Severn's private quarters and the vault protecting the Green-Wheely, Rachel turned to her brother for guidance before taking any further steps.

The antechamber was obstructed from view in the pledging pit below, but once they arrived backstage the siblings could see to the end of the twenty-foot tunnel-like hallway because light was emanating from the private chamber. Ray became fixated on a sleeping Severn, who was so still that his chamber could have been mistaken for a dilapidated mausoleum. Rachel, on the other hand, was keenly aware of their entire surroundings, and she thought she could make out the contours of another raccoon leaning against the wall not far from where Severn was sleeping.

Ray began to have second thoughts about leading Rachel to the Green-Wheely, and he considered leaving her to her own devices. After all, Rachel had made her own nest. She'd likely be caught, and although she'd plead for forgiveness from their father, Severn would make sure she was kicked out. Rachel would be off his back for good.

At that moment, Rachel caught wind of an opportunity. Below them, she spied an older raccoon emerging from the pledging pit who seemed poised to mount the front staircase of the mezzanine. Rachel telegraphed to Ray to look at what was happening. The old raccoon was trying to slip past the rotation of the Sentries undetected, and just as he reached the top of the staircase, Seth barreled down the antechamber and traveled another thirty feet to nab him.

The clickety-clack of Seth's overgrown claws scratching the metal

A Pledge's Father Headed for Detention

stage and the old raccoon's yelp at being apprehended, alerted the Sentries, who had just showed up embarrassingly late for the grave-yard shift. Ray remained completely motionless and listened to Seth browbeat the Sentries and warn them about distemper. Seth then turned his attention to the emaciated raccoon. It was crazy to think he would even contemplate entering Severn's chamber; he must have been suffering from some kind of madness.

Severn was woken up and startled by the disturbance, but Seth had the situation under control. He had already ordered Ray's father to hold the perpetrator in case they had to eliminate him and evacu-ate – only the Walkies were a greater threat than distemper. Naively, Ray thought it was cool his father was called to take the prisoner cap-tive. In truth, security protocols dictated that Severn and Seth be pro-tected at all costs, which meant that even the other Advisors were expendable.

Once Ray's father gave the all clear, Seth, Severn, and half of the Inner Guard joined him and the old raccoon in the open pledg-ing area. Ray's blood raced with excitement, for he had never seen a take down before! Certain that Rachel would be impressed with their father's police work, he suddenly realized he was talking to himself. He looked around frantically until he saw movement in the direction of the antechamber. Rachel was standing at the far end of it and had infiltrated Severn's private quarters!

As soon as Rachel could make eye contact with Ray, she gestured with her hands for him to come quickly and assist her. Ray was trembling as he ran through the antechamber unimpeded. As far as he knew, no one but Seth had ever been inside this room of Severn's. It wasn't ornate, but it was cavernous and could house an entire company of raccoons. The vault was located to one side, set back in a recessed area, but very close to Severn's resting place. Fortuitously, they could access the Green Wheely because the vault door hadn't been closed. Rachel then mounted the Green-Wheely, and she whispered in hushed tones to prevent her voice from echoing.

"I've got both my hands on the handle, but I need leverage. I'm not heavy enough to do the Turn alone," Rachel was panting. "We've got to work together."

Dreading the Inner Guard's imminent return, Ray worried that his father would disown him for trespassing in a restricted zone that contained such sensitive organic material. Worse, Ray's father might be indicted for Ray's insubordination. His anxiety morphed into panic as it dawned on him that he had brought a female whose pheromones could turn the Severnites' Lair into a powder keg!

Rachel hissed at her brother to snap out of his freak-out session and tip the Green-Wheely on her count. Ray gave her the push she needed, and she timed her fall with the force of gravity. Her grip never wavered, and the acrobatic swing of her body made the Turn possible. This had been coined a "mission-impossible" by the Pledges, but now his eccentric sister had conquered the Green-Wheely. Rachel had already concluded that despite the weight advantage of all the young adult males, no raccoon could open the Green-Wheely independently.

Rachel and Ray stood for a moment stunned by what they had accomplished. It was almost anti-climactic when the bin fell over and Rachel popped open the lid. Without anyone to witness their feat, Ray felt robbed of a victory. However, the noise they had created had not gone unnoticed, and Seth recognized another crisis in the making. Without a full regiment of Sentries present and the Master too groggy to ascertain a potential decoy, Seth's eyes sharpened. He yelled at the two Advisors to quit laughing at Ray's father, who looked clownishly oversized next to the scrawny raccoon in his custody.

"Fools! Get back to our Master's chamber, now!" Rachel flinched at the sound of Seth's command, and without a moment's hesitation, she escaped back out through the antechamber and deftly ran down the rear staircase. The Advisors arrived soon after in Severn's private quarters to witness the opened Green-Wheely lying next to a disoriented Ray, little more than a spectator caught up in the whirlwind of

Ray, "The Great Turner"

events.

Seth was the last Advisor to arrive, and he immediately lunged at Ray, but his claw fell short of its mark. Severn had caught Seth's paw mid-swing and held it until he disarmed Seth's fury. Severn's stare simultaneously communicated his thanks and reestablished his position as the alpha. Seth would not bite the hand that fed him, the hand that had mastered the Turn. Once he regained his senses, Seth began to think how absurd it was that this boy had opened the Green-Wheely on his own. Had there been an accomplice?

Meanwhile, Severn looked upon this disruption as something serendipitous.

"How delicious!" Severn gushed, and then he fixed his eyes ever so briefly on the Pledge's hapless father who had been carted in after the Advisors and Sentries had secured his room. "You really can't teach an old dog new tricks. Actually, he's as clumsy as an ox."

Severn then turned his attention to Ray. "But what do we have here! The precocious pup achieves the impossible: he opens the Green-Wheely right under the noses of my, what, highly trained security team?"

"The future, Seth, belongs to the youth! Hahaha. Take two Sentries and escort the old-timer to the D-block."

The Pledges had been schooled to believe the letter D stood

for "Detention," but it was actually code for "Death." The Advisors thought it best the Pledges be spared the truth of Severn's double-speak to protect the Master's reputation.

"Ray, *my boy!*" Severn glowed, "You have exceeded everyone's expectations and have now become the commander of your father's battalion."

Ray was quite taken with Severn's overtures but stopped short of celebrating when he noticed his father's long face. Ray's father said nothing and felt disappointed that he hadn't been there when his son accomplished this incredible feat. It was a poignant moment and yet Ray's father felt obsolete. Severn appeared to have become his boy's father figure.

Perhaps it was karma he was losing a son to Severn because Ray's father had sneered at the other fathers who were foolishly proud of their sons' abilities. Now, he had to admit that he empathized with them because they had sacrificed their sons by having them conscripted to the Severnites. When he noticed Ray was staring at him, he pulled himself together and stopped second-guessing himself. The Severnites were pragmatic, they would achieve the greater good, and they would make believers out of more raccoons yet.

With the Green-Wheely's inner contents spilled out in plain view, the Sentries had begun to salivate. Claiming the booty was the furthest thing from Ray's mind because he was consumed by fear that he would be exposed as a fraud. When Ray met his father's gaze, his eyes expressed a vulnerability he had never seen before in his tough dad. Ray couldn't imagine commanding him in battle. He didn't know a thing about fighting tactics. He didn't know any Pledges well enough who would protect him from harm. Not like his family. And where had Rachel gone? Would she be caught? Would she be OK?

Severn wouldn't let Ray shy away or feign humility over his accomplishment. Severn needed a poster-boy. He could count on the Sentries to hold the line because they were already battle-hardened. But almost all the Pledges had been sheltered, even hovered over by families who had pinned their hopes on their sons to succeed in Severn's de facto military academy.

More problematic was that they lacked grit, which meant they could turn tail at the first sign of blood. At last, Severn had the solution: Ray would play the part of a young commander, who, with just his magnetic presence, could prevent companies from splitting into disarray. While Ray beat the drum of war, Severn would direct his forces as Visionary and Brigadier-General of the Severnites.

Seth found all this nauseating. He hated how Ray's father was now "untouchable" because his son was being groomed as the Severnites' hero. As Severn became consumed with propaganda,

Seth stepped up as party whip. If Ray's father hadn't helped his son open the Green-Wheely, someone else had! Seth quietly ordered two Sentries to round up the best trackers of the Inner Guard. He pretended to direct a perimeter recon due to the earlier intrusion, but his real focus was to catch Ray's unknown accomplice, deliver the truth, and be vindicated.

The Wrath of Chester

Rachel Feels She Is to Blame

Chapter 9

Chester

Rachel had little time to lose. She, and especially Ray, would be coming home much later than usual, and their mother would sense something momentous had happened and insist on an explanation. Rachel's narrow escape had put a nervous jolt of energy into her tired legs, but the voice that had sounded the alarm back in Severn's chamber was tormenting her to run even faster. Although she didn't recognize this voice, she intuited that it belonged to a mentally disturbed or more vicious raccoon than Severn, and one that she should avoid at all costs.

Rachel was upset she had left Ray to fend for himself. She was like the bear who selfishly stirs up a bees' nest without first warning other bears nearby. Rachel was so concerned that Ray was still trapped in Severn's Lair that she couldn't absolve herself of guilt until he was running beside her and cursing like a marmot on Groundhog Day.

When she stopped to catch her breath and look back down the

street, she saw two raccoons approaching from the distance. From the safety of a bush, she extended her snout in their direction and tried to pick up Ray's scent and possibly their father's. She didn't recognize the raccoons' movement patterns as they ran in and out of the banks of driveways. They would periodically pause and then resume with quick bursts of speed. Ray knew his way home and wouldn't hesitate.

"That's weird, Ray never sniffs familiar driveways," thought Rachel. That's when she realized she was being hunted.

While Rachel feared for her life, Severn could not have felt more mastery over his destiny. He had been waiting for the right moment, the divine spark, to send his forces out and decimate the obstinate raccoon populations in corners of the city. He had amassed enough Pledges now to eliminate his rivals and their loyal families as long as the campaign was swift, and he had control of the minds and stomachs of his soldiers. He had promised the Severnites riches far greater than the contents of his Green-Wheely. That was the carrot. Now, Severn would show the unsophisticated raccoons the stick. The skirmish over the Green-Wheely in the morning had given Severn material for his most magnificent call-to-action that night.

The Yard Guard Attacks

"Brave Severnites," he commanded as day turned into night, "the pledging has concluded." Blank faces stared back in disbelief, but before any fathers or their bristling sons could speak out, Severn returned their exasperated looks with a decree.

"There is One among you who has succeeded. He now joins me as a superior raccoon who can outwit the Walkies. Do not envy him. His role comes with great responsibility, and he will lead one of our four battalions alongside his father. He is the Chosen One." The audience was now captivated.

"He has shown he can sublimate his hunger into constructive pursuits that will ensure we are cured of overpopulation. The Walkies promulgated overpopulation. The Walkies underestimate us. They think we haven't the intelligence to undo the harm they have caused us."

There were silent nods and fathers began to pat their sons on their backs, mimicking the physical affection their leader had bestowed on his protégé.

"I give you, Ray, The Great Turner, a champion who has emerged to inspire his generation to embrace the evolution of our species." The applause was cautious but supportive.

"The outliers who haven't pledged will now be conquered. They are inferior, and they won't put up much of a fight against the Walkies, much less my worthy Severnites!" The crowd that had amassed around the Master let out a simultaneous and formidable screech.

"We will put those furry nincompoops out of their misery. While Ray and my Advisors confirm our plans for the imminent blitzkrieg, my Sentries will put you into companies that will form the battalions run by my Advisors. Henceforth, they are your Generals, and the Sentries who've presided over the pledging, your Captains. We have risen like the Walkies. We have cut the umbilical cord that subjected us to the whims of Mother Nature. We are the Rangers of the Night and will wash our hands in blood!"

Rachel ran up the family's Red Oak tree like her tail was on fire. She was overcome with emotion. She had done it. She was the family's Turner. At the same time, she agonized over having possibly jeopardized her brother's freedom and complicated matters for their father, which would mean neither of them could help defend the family from what was coming.

Rose was awakened by her daughter's sobbing and jarred into thinking it was time to feed Rory and Ralph. Rachel had the smell of the spoils on her, but she looked miserable hunched over with

Seth Orders the Kill

her back to her mother. Either Rachel's scent or her weeping would attract some unwanted attention if this kept up.

"What in the world?! Should we all wake up and feed before the dog barks?" asked Rose, oblivious to the gravity of the situation. With Rachel still unable to speak, Rose now guessed something dreadfully wrong had happened. Had Rose been mistaken to give Rachel and Ray her qualified blessing? She had strongly protested against the dangers of them going it alone, but she had also become so impressed with their bravery and degree of care that she acquiesced and let them attempt to open a Green-Wheely.

Rachel broke her silence at last, "Mother, I, I, I, . . . I opened a Green-Wheely with Ray tonight."

At this, Rose felt a flood of relief and then celebrated her children's success by taking Rachel's hands in hers and jumping up and down as best a mature mother raccoon can. Rachel and Ray had gone out and done it! Her children had mastered the Turn. Rachel met her mother's joy with ambivalence and interrupted the jumping with a blunt warning.

"Mother! It wasn't any old Green Wheely. It belongs to Severn, and he was using it to trick raccoons into amassing an army."

Rachel skipped a beat and then resumed, "Help me wake the others. I think I've put the family in grave danger!"

Rose had never seen Rachel's expression so anguished and resolute, so she yelled at Ricky to get the boys up immediately. Ralph was last to leave the Red Oak's tree-fork den, and he was just in time, for Seth had arrived with his two expert trackers and three other Sentries. This tactical unit had completely cut off the family from escape. The fence line was no longer an option, so Ricky rushed the youngins back up the tree to its highest branches while Rose and Rachel remained on the lowest boughs to defend.

"You stink of duplicity," raged Seth. "Come out, coward! Hiding your identity among the others, are you?" He then adjusted the cadence in his voice, using long pauses between sentences that increased the tension and achieved his intent to intimidate.

"Give up the perpetrator, and no harm will come to the rest of you," which was a blatant lie; they'd all have to die because Seth couldn't be sure which raccoon had infiltrated the Lair.

Rose roared back, "Over my dead body!" The verbal threats went back and forth just long enough for the Yard Guard, Chester the English Mastiff, to perk up from his bed by the kitchen door. Chester then demanded that his owner, a local politician, let him out in the backyard where the magnificent Red Oak stood.

Seth was not intimidated by Rose or her nursery of raccoons, for he had admirable fighting qualities and a swagger that kept his rivals at bay. In truth, he was a city cull survivor, deported to the country-side, but he came back thanks to his single-minded ferocity. Seth had incredible determination, especially when locked on a kill. He instructed his Sentries to ascend the tree and not return until they brought back the head of the conspirator to Severn.

Unfortunately for Seth, his tunnel vision caused him to be blind-sided by Chester, who deftly lunged at Seth's neck, bit into his jugu-lar, and ended his life with a sharp snap over the canine's expansive shoulders. The Sentries turned around and descended on the Yard Guard, but the first two were no match for the dog's strength and were mauled to death. The third managed to hold on to the Yard Guard's fleshy face long enough to allow the two trackers to join the struggle and strike with all their might to bring the giant down.

The Battle of the Severnites

A Sentry Engages in War

Chapter 10

Causing a Commotion

The altercation with the Yard Guard allowed the family of raccoons to escape from their tree and traverse the fence line. Their silent and orderly evacuation was in stark contrast to the Sentries' bombastic fight. No raccoon dared to look back, so none of them knew of Chester's demise. The politician couldn't figure out who'd done it because he had closed the sliding door behind his dog when he let him out. Startled by the cries of the slaughter, he pulled the door open again to find his backyard littered with three raccoon corpses and his lifeless English Mastiff.

With the door still open, the kitchen light was reflected in the eyes of the three Sentries looking back at him. The politician grabbed the push broom from the corner of his deck and swung it wildly at the raccoons to scare them off, which sent two of them running. The last raccoon tried to flee but failed to pull himself over the fence and succumbed to his wounds. He ended up slouched over in a corner of the yard as dark, thick liquid oozed from his body.

Back at Severn's Lair, the military campaign was rapidly progressing, and Severn had begun instructing his Advisors to assemble their battalions into attack formation. Although disappointed at missing his son's momentous Turn, Ray's father put it behind him and planted a celebratory bear hug on Ray, and for the moment, father and son could enjoy their embrace. As it happened, the Sentries assigned to Ray's father had left with Seth, which meant his battalion's launch was delayed until Seth and those Sentries returned.

Seth's recon was so ill-timed that Severn was losing patience with the remaining Inner Guard. In order to launch the campaign, Severn decided to remake his battle plan with the remaining two Advisors and three Sentries so that their companies of Pledges formed two new wrecking crews. Their mission was made simpler and more brutal: bludgeon to death any unsuspecting raccoon going about its regular business and corral any escapees into the centre of town. Ray's battalion would then come up the middle when Seth showed up, capitalize on the ensuing panic, and kettle them.

Ray's father knew Severn's tirade wasn't good for morale – none of the rank and file had ever seen such anger coming from Severn. Ray's father quietly instructed Ray to gather up their Pledges at once, but he suggested that Ray let him lead the third wave. Ray happily complied because this would restore his father's pride and take the pressure off Ray to command the Pledges and their fathers. Ray had never been part of a mission before, and this was feeling like things were about to get ugly.

Ray enthusiastically participated in the preparation exercises, thumping his chest in unison with his battalion, lying in wait for Severn's call. When Ray's father explained that Seth's battalion would represent the fourth and final wave, Ray suddenly remembered that Seth had disappeared shortly after his sister had gone. Had he thumped his chest too hard, or was the anguish he was now experiencing the result of hiding the truth from his father?

One after another, the Pledge's fathers came to congratulate Ray and his father on their accomplishment and offer well wishes for the fight ahead. Ray's father reminded them that after the war he and his talented son would teach them to open the Green-Wheelies and increase their personal fortunes.

"Visualize all those Green Wheelies filled with delectable treats to push our battalion to victory!" urged Ray's father, surprised by his own eloquence. Motivated by their trusted leader, the battalion could barely wait for news of Seth's return.

Ray's father had profound admiration for his son and thought to himself, "Just look at him now. Our family's first Turner!" He added aloud, "Ray, you've inspired the Severnites. See how your example has revved up our soldiers? I couldn't be prouder. We're on the right side of history."

"Father . . ." Ray's voice was barely audible.

Ray's father interrupted him, "Because you were first from the womb, your mother and I had always imagined wonderful days ahead of you, but could we have predicted this? No!" Getting carried away in the moment, he now strutted over to Ray, and like a juvenile gang member looking for a piece of the action he threw his arm around Ray's shoulders.

"Between us, how'd you do it?" After a long pause, he was done teasing his son and spoke again. "C'mon, son, I'm kidding. Really. Starting with the Occupation, all the Advisors and Sentries will be trained on the Green-Wheely."

Severn's plan was to disband the Inner Guard and reward each member with an administrative branch to keep stock of the Walkies' trade in castoffs. Besides making them happy with instant wealth and status, Severn could count on their loyalty because they would be married to the nascent economy, a consumerist class hooked on his promises of affluence and lives of comfort.

"Father, Rachel's the one." Ray had finally mustered up the

A Raccoon Fatality in the City

courage to confess. "You've *missed* her again – tonight!"

Ray's father was so consumed by tactical planning and keeping the troops' spirits high that he failed to take in Ray's words. Also, his daughter's achievements were not foremost in his mind, so he failed to notice Rachel's development as the family's true champion.

"Severn has rigged the pledge," Ray continued. "No one can open the Green-Wheely alone – it depends on the help of another – Rachel showed me."

This was stunning news. Almost as stunning as the realization that Severn had come up the central staircase with a large number of Pledges in tow. Everyone had heard what Ray said, so Severn calmly extricated himself from the clingy Pledges who still idolized him and took to the front of the stage once more to address Ray's claim.

"Ray, *my boy*, you've surprised me again, but this time it's with your candour. Would your partner like to come forward to teach us the Turn?"

Severn's sadistic streak surfaced as he felt his grip on power slipping, so he threatened Ray and his father with a despicable low blow in a simpering tone, "My Pledges have not seen their girlfriends in a very long time, and they might take a fancy to Ms. Rachel."

The Severnites on the eastern and western flanks had been making progress towards the city's centre. They sustained heavy losses in the east as they ran into an unusually high number of coyotes in the ravines they crossed. However, the Severnites from the west had nearly reached the city centre, and both battalions felt confident that the reinforcements from the north would finish off any remaining raccoons who thought they could still cheat death.

The Battle of the Severnites caused such a commotion that it literally lit up the town. The Walkies were rudely awakened; their bedroom lights dotted the local streets and cast a faint glow everywhere the dreadful screeching was heard, which included gardens, berms, bushes, trees, verandas, sheds, garages, alleyways, and beneath cars.

Never had there been this much carnage in one night since the burning down of the city at the time of its founding over two centuries ago. The information phone lines were tied up and the Internet portal crashed; Animal Services was taken completely unaware. But the extraordinary number of complaints about the raccoon frenzy was not as big a factor in meting out punishment as the death of Chester the Yard Guard. His owner, the City Councillor, was profoundly angry at the animals, and he made his Constituency Assistant call his allies on Council to repay him a "favour" that would manifest as a municipal retaliation.

At Severn's Lair, another momentous turn of events had taken place as Ray's father exclaimed, "Rose!" and he stood there looking at the back of the mezzanine like he had seen a ghost. Emerging from the top of the same rear staircase that her children had used in their heist, Rose came into full view of Severn.

"Rose?" Severn cackled in derision. "Dearest Advisor, is that your final word before you perish? How quaintly appropriate, my sentimental friend, for you shall be buried alongside a rose."

Severn wasn't the least bit threatened by Ray's father, who had struck a fearsome Sumo stance. Although his father's powerful pose gave Ray courage, he could not dispute the math of being outnumbered by the Pledges crowded around their Master. Severn would have written the father and son duo's epitaphs if Rose hadn't retorted, "Funny, my husband claimed this place was a fortress. What a shame. No one to greet a lady and open the front door."

Severn thrust himself within inches of the matriarch, simultaneously circling and scrutinizing her as he spoke. "Not bad. Good bones. Someone had to give Ray the brains."

As Severn shot a scornful look at Ray's father to demoralize him, Rose dispelled the gloom with her ever-ready wit, giving her mate a

An Opportunistic City Councillor

quick wink to reassure him as she said, "You're right about the brains. I'm here for my boy."

From then on, the Pledges became audience members in a peanut gallery, well positioned to watch surprise after surprise unfold. The scene had created unintended entertainment value so that no Pledge was willing to interrupt because, deep down, all raccoons are thrill-seekers.

In true dramatic fashion, Rose had entered stage right whereas Rachel entered stage left from the other rear staircase. Now two females appeared before the Pledges, and Severn found himself outflanked by Rachel and Rose. Severn never flinched under pressure, but he was in unfamiliar territory and appeared weary. Backing up to the central staircase and front of the stage, he saw Rachel and Rose mirror his pivot with their backs towards their boys, eyes squarely on the peanut gallery.

Disgusted by the family reunion, Severn readied an order to kill to close out his sermon. Severn directly addressed the mother and daughter on stage.

"Ha! These sows have backed their insipid males into a corner. Females do little more than provide us offspring. You may think you are Nature's makers. Homemakers, maybe. But I will deliver you to your MAKER!"

To Severn's shock, there was barely a peep from his Pledges or their fathers. For this group of modest intellect, who had been raised and lived with females all their lives, Severn's command paralyzed them with cognitive dissonance. They were like deer caught in the headlights, and there was an awkward silence of blank stares, then puzzled faces, and then helter-skelter thoughts: "Where did these other raccoons come from? Will the Master destroy them all by himself? Does he mean to kill a mother who stood up for her boy? Punish the family of a Turner? Who's going to take out that big Advisor? Wait, did Ray get the Turn on account of his father?! He ain't a hero after all. Ray's accomplice is pretty, is she single?"

These unfocused murmurings filled Severn's Lair, and the room was falling into disarray. Over the last months, some Pledges had taken a real liking to the General, Ray's father, because he said their sacrifice would bring honour and relief to their families. Others in their battalion just found a change in command refreshing. Ray's father's orders didn't come with all that flowery language that Severn chided them with, either.

Severn sensed he would not be able to reclaim control unless he took drastic action. Of the four raccoons who dared to defy his power, Rose was the closest mark and became the target of his wrath. There was a collective gasp upon seeing Rose lying at the feet

The Tempest Swallows Its Leader

of their Master, who showed the unmistakable crimson of murder on his face.

Before Ray's father could retaliate, Ray and two more mutineering fathers and sons had torn into Severn. Ray's father braced himself and became an impassable barrier to thwart loyal Severnites from saving Severn. This allowed Ray to end Severn's life, but no one knew he had been slain due to a torrent of dust swallowing up the stage area. A massive fight had broken out between two thirds of the Pledges and their fathers who believed their Master still needed saving; the other third were sympathetic to the General, who exuded tangible leadership qualities and old-fashioned family values.

Oh, the sound! The fury! Because thirty raccoons were locked in combat, even Ray's father got tossed from the fray. When he got back up, he was elated to see that his children had draped their mother over their shoulders so that she could walk on her hind legs. Rose had sustained severe trauma to her front right arm – an open fracture. Luckily, she had lifted her paw just in time to block Severn's all-or-nothing bite to her neck.

After Severn's demise, Ray broke through the thick cloud of dust to reach Rachel, who was struggling to get under and support their mother's weight and move her out of harm's way. As Ray helped Rachel lift their mother and find an exit, they were arrested by the family patriarch's booming voice.

"Go. I've got this. Go! I love you all!"

Rose at Peace

Chapter 11

Cherry Blossoms

The family of raccoons had endured some very trying times. While still grieving the loss of their father, the accidental death of Ralph a few months later bore heavy on the hearts of the remaining members, particularly their mother. But it was thanks to a raccoon named George, who had befriended Ray when they were Pledges, that the family had finally decided to make a fresh start and migrate to the largest park in the city. George had been raised in this park, which had an unparalleled tree canopy, and he told Rose she must come to see the beauty of the falling petals in spring. The family listened carefully to George's account of how the park was once overrun with coyotes, but following the Battle of the Severnites and the Great Cull the park had become hospitable again to many animals, especially the hares.

George had encouraged Ray and his siblings to gain consensus before relocating, and thanks to his wise counsel he became the family's lynchpin. Ray asked Ricky to consider whether a new home might ease their mother's depression. After Ricky gave his two thumbs up, Ray felt the family could cope with a move again. They settled in the city park that George recommended, and Rachel noticed the change in their mother almost immediately, as she became much more engaged and observant. For example, Rose was tickled pink by how Rory was evolving from a lad who would immediately fall upon any food at hand to one who would insist that nobody eat until his de facto guardian Ricky had come home.

In some ways, Rory resembled his father in that he was stubbornly loyal and fought for what was in his family's best interests. To anyone who would listen, Rory would gleefully defend his view that "Green-Wheely casserole tastes better when everyone's here to share it."

"Once Rory makes up his mind . . . " Rose chuckled to herself, "Well, the new tree burl worked out after all."

She felt the cool morning breeze graze her nose, which made the dewy liquid on it sparkle, and now her sense of smell informed her that not only Ricky but also Rachel and Ray were nearing the foot of their Sakura tree, which was in full splendour. The siblings had come to take Rory out for foraging practice.

Ray never failed to be impressed by the enormity of the surrounding Walkies' homes and how they generated a never-ending

George, the Family Friend

source of food. Rachel was content that the Walkies left them alone, and since these trees towered above the park, their dogs never paid them much attention either. Ricky had an eye for tree burls, and he reclaimed a knot for him and Rory to keep cool in the daytime.

Had Severn survived that fateful outburst in his Lair, he would have been mortified to see his reign snuffed out by the Walkies. Little did he know, it was Seth who had caused half of the city's raccoons to lose their lives. In his zeal to purge the Severnites of infiltrators, Seth had inadvertently caused the budding empire to fall like dominos when his Sentries had violated the unspoken boundary of killing a living member of a Walkies' household. While his Sentries could be forgiven for defending themselves because they behaved like any other animal when cornered, Seth was blinded by his devotion to the Master and satisfying his need to be right. If Seth had not been so wrapped up in self-righteous wrath, he might have realized he'd picked the wrong yard to settle his scores because Chester belonged to a city councillor in need of scoring political points in an election year.

Once the city ordinance authorizing raccoon extermination was passed, the battle-weary Severnites and surviving victims of the war were trapped and euthanized in what became known to survivors as "The Great Cull." Animal Services cautiously handled the extraordinary amount of dead and injured raccoons, who had been reported to have rabies, distemper, or some combination of the two. Unofficially, the city administration blamed a rise in the number of coyotes for beating up the raccoons this way, but the civil workers suspected that the coyote explanation was politically motivated. Their union was cynical about any last minute decision coming from management. In the court of public opinion, however, the city councillor had the prescience and therefore the authority to clean up their town.

Yet complicating matters for the ambitious councillor was a young environmentalist's viral SicSock video of pre-army Severn and Seth tipping a green bin and nabbing its contents. The talented videographer used his cell phone footage of master and disciple opening the new generation of green-bin receptacles and synced it with an audio version of the clownish jingle, Pickety Max. So it was that Severn and Seth went down in history as the raccoons who humiliated the savvy politician, who found himself in hot water due to a garbage strike later that spring and tens of thousands of views of raccoons helping themselves to the festering problem.

Young adults across the city were abuzz with the fresh new social media campaign inspired by the activist's raccoon video, and they were determined to hold leaders like the city councillor to account. Frustrated that their climate march had not resulted in more signifi-cant and fast-paced change, they were outraged over inheriting the junk heap of unchecked materialism from the older folks. They would expose anybody they saw greenwashing environmental stewardship.

"Hey, hey, HEY! Don't be fighting like chickens in a coop," Rachel shouted at Ray and George to quit playing around and focus on the upcoming Turns at hand. She often teased them about what hap-pens when too many male raccoons gather in one place. Beyond the thicket along the border of their park were the swollen Green-Wheelies and excess debris slumping next to them. The smell was irresistible! It wasn't summer yet, but the public had taken to the air-waves to complain about a new situation arising from the garbage workers' strike. Not only had the green bin waste continued to accu-mulate, but also the significantly smaller raccoon population meant less of it was being consumed. As a result, the Green-Wheelies' con-tents had runneth over.

That evening, Rose was delighted to hear the tree banter filter-ing through the leaves after Ricky, Rachel, George, and Ray returned as heroes with partially-eaten hard-boiled eggs and halves of rotten avocados they had stuffed into malleable styrofoam containers with greasy noodles still clinging to the insides. Rory had been sleeping peacefully curled up in her lap for the last two hours. Now that Ricky had come home, Rory was quick to his feet and followed George and his older siblings to Rats' Alley to grab dessert.

Having survived the Great Cull, Rose was at peace watching her family grow up into fine individuals whom she knew would take care of each other. The apex predators like the hawks were happy, too, and she had to admit her mate had been right to uproot. She was no longer enamoured with the countryside that had been transformed by highways and subdivisions.

Tonight, Rose would depart before her children came back from their second foray. The gentle breeze had lifted the Sakura petals from the boughs above and then let them flutter to the ground in a carpet of pink. As she breathed her last, many petals came to rest on Rose, forming a soft contour around her body like the first snowfall on gentle hills that shelter sleeping valleys.

Ray Settles In

Author

Marc Yamaguchi is an English professor with Centennial College in Toronto, Canada. He did his Masters in Environmental Education and Communication. He is also an avid rain gardener and enjoys freelance writing when his family gives him permission to go down rabbit holes. Arai Guma is his first published work of fiction.

Illustrator

Hung Hong (a.k.a Bom) is a toy designer/ illustrator who creates characters, illustrations and toys that bring fun to everyone. He has a passion for the humorous and lighthearted side of designs with a knack for putting unique spins on his works.

BANG!
CLANG!

LIFE CAN BE UNFAIR, AND DAD SUFFERED A CRUELER HUMILIATION AGAINST THE IMPREGNABLE GREEN BIN.

UGGGGGGH... ALMOST... GOT IT...

PARADISE WAS LOST, BUT RED-TAILED HAWK WOULDN'T BE CAUGHT DEAD MIGRATING WITH THE EARTH-BOUND CREATURES.

FORTUNE IS SHIFTING IN OUR FAVOUR...

...A GREAT MANY OF YOU MAY NOT HAVE BECOME A TURNER, BUT YOU ARE NONETHELESS SOLIDERS...

...WHO WILL GUARANTEE OUR VICTORY OVER THIS CONCRETE JUNGLE.

... WE HAVE EVOLVED FROM OUR FOREST FORAGING COUSINS WHO HAVE A NAIVE VIEW OF THE WALKIES' BENEVOLENCE.

WE WILL TAKE BACK THE NIGHT!

YAH!
YAH!
YAH!
YAH!
YAH!

THAT'S WHAT I'M TALKIN' ABOUT!

www.ingramcontent.com/pod-product-compliance
Lightning Source LLC
Chambersburg PA
CBHW070401200726
48294CB00003B/1023